S0-ACZ-413

Legends of Earth Air Fire and Water

by Eric and Tessa Hadley

illustrated by Bryna Waldman

CAMBRIDGE UNIVERSITY PRESS

Cambridge
New York   New Rochelle
Melbourne   Sydney

Other legends books from Cambridge

Legends of the Sun and Moon by Eric and Tessa Hadley

Legends of the Animal World by Rosalind Kerven

The Shining Stars by Ghislaine Vautier and Kenneth McLeish

The Way of the Stars by Ghislaine Vautier and Kenneth McLeish

The Seven Wonders of the World by Kenneth McLeish

Published by the Press Syndicate of the University of Cambridge
The Pitt Building, Trumpington Street, Cambridge CB2 1RP
32 East 57th Street, New York, NY 10022, USA
10 Stamford Road, Oakleigh, Melbourne 3166, Australia

First published 1985
Reprinted 1988

Printed in Hong Kong

Library of Congress catalogue card number: 84–12089

British Library cataloguing in publication data

Hadley, Eric
Legends of earth, air, fire and water.
1. Tales 2. Legends
I. Title II. Hadley, Tessa
398.2   PZ8.1

ISBN 0 521 26311 5

CONTENTS

ABOUT THE STORIES

When you have read these stories it might be interesting to read them to someone else, and then ask them to guess where the story-tellers come from. You can sense from the stories how important fire was to people who had to live through the long winter nights of the far North, or how precious water was to the original inhabitants of Australia.

The stories tell of the great, basic forces without which life would not be possible: earth, air, fire and water. But the stories also introduce us to the knowledge of these peoples. The story-tellers knew their world, all the plants and animals, the movement and changes of the seasons, with a detail which only comes from knowing how much your daily life depends upon them. To take the knowledge for granted could lead to disaster. For forces as strong as fire, the winds or water are treacherous and difficult to control – drought changes to flood, soft balmy days are broken by storms.

Most of you reading these stories will live in cities or towns. There the earth is buried deep underneath roads and pavements. Sometimes it might show itself round the edges of a lawn, or carefully planted and fenced in a park. A lot of the time you'll live indoors. Your water will come from a tap. You'll have a fire possibly, but no flames. And the indoor breeze might even come from a regular, quietly whirring machine.

Earth, air, fire and water – these are things for holidays. Then, briefly, we may meet and feel them in a different way. It may begin to dawn on you that your tame tap water is a distant relative of the icy, rushing stream you cross or the wave that smacks into you on the beach.

With the earth beneath your feet – your bare feet perhaps – you walk a little differently. In the open, and away from rooms and streets the air moves freely, and you have to move with it and in it. Sometimes it tears at you and freezes you to the bone. Other times, it warms and gently supports you.

Now we begin to get a glimpse of a bigger world and we have to adjust the way we look at things. It's like someone suddenly walking from a darkened room into bright sunshine, or like the people in our story from Polynesia who stand upright to watch a marvellous world they had never guessed at open up above them.

The peoples who told the stories in this collection did not live in towns or cities. What we have done with earth, air, fire and water they would have found, *did* find, hard to understand. It's worth remembering too that many of the peoples who told these stories no longer live as they did then, if they still exist at all. That is because the way we choose to live destroyed or is destroying their way of life. We have two stories which belong to the Cree and Iroquois peoples of North America. It was a great leader of another Indian nation, the Sioux, who said, when he first visited a city, 'They had forgotten that the earth was their mother . . . even the grass they keep in prison.'

POLYNESIA

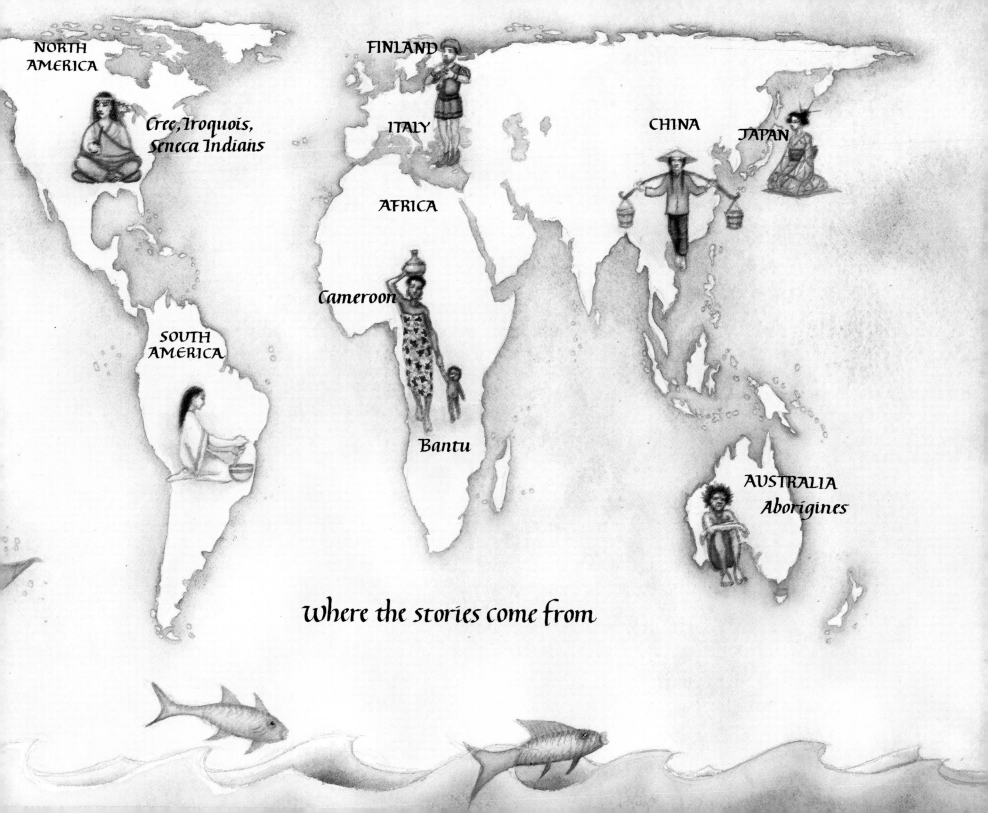

NORTH
AMERICA

Cree, Iroquois,
Seneca Indians

FINLAND

ITALY

AFRICA

CHINA

JAPAN

Cameroon

SOUTH
AMERICA

Bantu

AUSTRALIA
Aborigines

Where the stories come from

A BIT OF EARTH

Day after day, night after night, it had rained. When the rain finally stopped Weesack-Kachak did not move. Now nothing was left except for Weesack-Kachak; and Otter, Beaver and Muskrat who had climbed up onto Weesack-Kachak's body and floated with him on the flood.

Water . . . it had even seeped into Weesack-Kachak's brain. It filled his mind and drowned all his tricks and schemes. But the rain had stopped and, like a breeze stirring the water, a voice sounded in Weesack-Kachak's dreams:

'I warned you. "Take good care of my world," I said. "Do not trick the animals and people I have made. Do not let them fight and quarrel or I will take everything away and wash the earth clean." '

Weesack-Kachak shivered and his companions started uneasily in their watery dreams.

'The rain has stopped,' he said. And he began to hope.

'Try again, Weesack-Kachak,' said the voice. 'See what you can make of the old earth that I have covered with water. Believe me, I shall give you nothing new.'

For the first time, Weesack-Kachak noticed Otter, Beaver and Muskrat.

'Otter,' he whispered, 'you are brave, strong and quick. Slip into the water, and bring me a bit of earth. I will make an island for us. Do it, Otter, and I will see that you have plenty of fish to eat.'

So Otter dived – three times he slipped into the water but he failed each time to find any earth.

Weesack-Kachak shouted at the exhausted Otter.

'Weakling! Coward! Not like you, Beaver. You are so strong you can dive straight down to the bottom of the flood and bring me back a bit of the old earth. Do it, brave Beaver, and I'll build you a house on the island where you'll be warm all winter.'

How Beaver tried – he wanted a warm winter home. But when they pulled his breathless body out after the third dive, he wanted nothing except not to go down again into the cold dark water.

'You are our last chance, Muskrat. Otter and Beaver are fools. They got lost. You may be small but I'll feed you up with the roots I'll make.'

So Muskrat jumped head first into the water and came back – with nothing. A second time he dived and was away much longer. When he returned Weesack-Kachak looked at his forepaws and sniffed:

'I smell the smell of earth. Try again, my brave Muskrat – just one little piece – straight down!'

Muskrat was away so long this time that Weesack-Kachak had given up all hope. Then he saw the bubbles coming up through the water and he reached his long arm down and dragged Muskrat out. He was almost dead but in his forepaws he was holding a piece of the old earth.

Weesack-Kachak seized it from him and in no time at all he had expanded the bit of earth into an island. Muskrat, Otter and Beaver rested after their efforts, while Weesack-Kachak wondered what to do next:

'I've got my bit of earth. Now with some wood and perhaps a few bones . . . Oh, Muskrat, this is no time for resting; we've only just begun.'

Cree Indian

with the earth *he* put up a notice in the village.

'What game do you think you're playing, Yasohachi?' said his master. 'Your field is still as lumpy as the back of a toad and yet you waste your time putting up this ridiculous notice: "On Sunday at four o'clock Yasohachi will climb from his field to heaven."'

But Yasohachi just smiled. 'I haven't got time to explain, master. I'm off to make the climb right now.'

Yasohachi marched off to his field and his master followed on behind, finding it hard to keep up with his pace.

A large crowd of villagers had already gathered in the field. They were milling about, peering at a long pole standing upright in the ground. They found it hard to keep steady on their feet – one foot would be up on a great lump of earth, while the other foot was down in a hole. Yasohachi pushed his way through and grasping the pole firmly with one hand he spoke to the crowd:

'Ladies and gentlemen. Watch closely. And forget nothing when you proudly tell your children and grandchildren that *you* were present on that famous Sunday when, at four o'clock, Yasohachi climbed from his field to heaven.'

He took hold of the pole with both hands and pulled himself up. He paused for a moment, reached

CLIMBING TO HEAVEN

It was early spring and soon it would be time for the rice to be planted. One by one the villagers began to prepare their fields. First the hard clumps of earth had to be broken up and the fields smoothed and ploughed. At last, only Yasohachi's field stood out, lumpy and uneven. While the other villagers worked and struggled

quicker than any of them. While they were still dusting themselves down, he had walked off a few paces and replanted the pole firmly in the earth. Up he want again – one pull, two pulls – he was over half way. But on the third pull the pole swayed, the crowd scattered, and down came Yasohachi.

Two hours later, the dusty, earth-spattered villagers were straggling back home.

'Didn't I say he'd never be able to do it?'

'It's not natural.'

'Climbing to heaven on a pole.'

Yasohachi and his master stood in the middle of the field alone.

'I think I'll start planting tomorrow.'

But his master just scowled. He scowled at Yasohachi and the now perfectly smooth field stretching out around them.

Japanese

up with his hands, and pulled again. A gasp went through the crowd as the pole began to lean. The next moment the villagers had scattered in all directions, running, stumbling and tripping over the uneven earth.

Most of them had already fallen to the ground as Yasohachi landed with a crash. But he was up

YHI BRINGS THE EARTH TO LIFE

There were no stars, no sun, no moon. The earth lay waiting, silent in the darkness. Nothing moved, no wind blew across the barren plain or the bare bones of the mountains. There was neither heat nor cold, alive or dead . . . nothing . . . waiting. Who knows how long?

Beyond the earth, Yhi lay waiting too, sleeping the long sleep. It was Baiame the great spirit who broke that sleep.

In the beginning, there was the sound of Baiame whispering across the universe:

'Yhi, awake.'

His whisper invaded her dreams.

'Yhi, awake.'

Her limbs stirred, her eyelids flickered and opened, and light shone from her eyes flooding across the plain and the mountains.

Yhi stepped down to earth and from that moment, where there had been nothing, there was everything – sound, movement, light.

The earth felt all these things; it woke at that first footstep. At each new step Yhi took it showed what it had dreamed throughout that long dark time. Flowers, trees, shrubs and grasses sprang up wherever she walked and when she finally stopped to rest the barren plain was lost under a sea of blooms.

As she rested Baiame whispered to her again:

'This is the beginning. The earth has shown you its beauty but without the dance of life it will not be complete. Take your light into the caves beneath the earth and see what will happen.'

The old darkness still ruled under the earth. There were no

seeds here to spring into life at her footstep. Instead her light reflected from metallic veins and sparkling opal points in the shadowy rock forms. As she moved the darkness reformed behind her and voices boomed and echoed:

'No, no no! Let us sleep, sleep, sleep.'

But Yhi never faltered and soon there were new sounds – faint clicks, scrapings and scratchings which grew louder and louder as the insects crept, flew and swarmed from every dark corner. Yhi's warmth coaxed them out and she led them up into the plain, into the waiting grass and leaves and flowers where their buzzing and chirruping drowned the dark wailing from below the earth.

This time Yhi did not pause. She strode across the plain while Baiame whispered:

'The ice caves in the mountains – take your light there.'

It seemed that Yhi had met her match in the cold blank silence. But somewhere there began the steady drip, drip, drip of water, free at last. Then, a cracking and crashing as great slabs of ice lost their freezing hold on the cave walls. The surface of the ice lakes splintered and new shapes broke through. These shapes flowed and wavered, unlike the dead ice lumps, and fish, snakes and reptiles were swept out to join the living earth outside as the lakes overflowed.

Yhi pressed on deeper but this time as she moved from cave to cave it was not solid, resisting ice she met but the touch of fur and feather. Birds and animals gathered to her and she led them out to add their voices to the new world.

'It is good. My world is alive,' Baiame said.

Aboriginal

NAMING THE WINDS

In the broad north sky lives the giant, Ga-oh. His great hands hold the reins of the four creatures who help him control the winds. When the world was made he called them to him in turn.

The first to come was Bear who pushed mountains aside as he lumbered along. Bear lowered his head when Ga-oh cried out:

'Bear, you are strong. Your cold breath freezes water and the

clasp of your broad arms could crush the whole earth. So be the North Wind and watch over my herd of winter winds when I let them loose in the sky.'

When Ga-oh had bound him with a leash, Bear prowled off to take his place in the north sky.

Ga-oh called again, but gently this time, his voice soft and warm as a summer breeze. The air was filled with the scent of flowers and the sound of birdsong as Fawn came proudly lifting her head:

'Fawn, you are gentle. You walk with the summer sun. So be the South Wind and watch my flock of summer winds in peace. Bend your head while I leash you, for you are swift and might escape me and return to the earth.'

Ga-oh's next cry spread an ugly darkness through the clouds. But they were torn apart by Panther's snarling answer as he sprang to meet Ga-oh, claws bared:

'Panther, ugly and fierce, you will fight the strong storms. You can carry the whirlwind on your strong back, and toss the great sea waves high in the air. So be the West Wind. In the west sky even the sun will hurry to hide when you howl your warning and no wind will dare stray when you snarl.'

Panther crept off to the west sky pulling at his leash.

But the earth has four corners and one was still empty, so Ga-oh called for the last time. As his cry died away a low moan spread through the air and the moan carried a chilling mist with it. There was the crash of branches breaking, the thud of hooves – nearer and nearer – until there, before Ga-oh, stood Moose.

Ga-oh spoke to Moose as he tied a strong leash round his neck:

'Moose, your breath blows the mist and the cold rain follows.

Your antlers break a path through the forest for my storms. So be the East Wind and your breath will chill the young clouds as they float through the sky.'

Ga-oh led Moose to his place in the east sky:

'Here you must stay forever.'

When he had chosen his helpers, Ga-oh returned to the broad north sky where he too must remain forever. If he is happy his fingers relax on Fawn's rein and warm south winds whisper to the earth. Sometimes he is restless and unbinds Bear so that strong winds whip up the sea and bend the forest trees. When Ga-oh longs to be free his anger grows and he ceases to struggle with Panther's leash. The West Wind whines and snarls – trees are uprooted, the streams are dashed into leaping furies, the sea waters rise like mountains . . .

But then he remembers that his duty is to keep the winds to their proper season and his hand tightens again on Panther's leash.

Iroquois

LIFTING THE SKY

When the sky rested on the land, life was hard for the people of the islands. They went about hunched over and cramped. If they lit a fire to cook their food, the smoke curled round the low roof of blue stone and hung there unable to escape. It filled their nostrils and made their eyes water.

This is how it was until one day the islanders were visited by Ru, who lived in the underworld.

Ru could not bear to see the people choking, their eyes streaming, so he said to his son, the great Maui:

'I'll help them. You and the men cut strong wooden stakes. I will push the sky away from the earth. As I take the strain, you must place the stakes upright and they will support the sky.'

When each man was ready with a long stake, Ru lay down on his back with his legs bent and his feet braced firmly against the blue stone sky.

'Ready?' he cried.

'Ready!' came the answer.

And with one mighty thrust Ru straightened his legs and the blue stone lifted away from the earth.

'The stakes! Quickly!' shouted Ru, trembling with the effort. In one movement they were in place: the blue stone shuddered, settled.

The people stood waiting, breathless. But it held, it held!

'Thank you, Ru! Ru, the Supporter of the Sky!' the people shouted.

'It was nothing. Really.'

It was hard to say who was more pleased at the work done that

day. The islanders could stand upright and move freely. Their eyes widened as they took in the light and space Ru had made for them, and as they breathed the fresh air for the first time.

As for Ru, he loved the praise of the islanders, and he came back to hear it again and again.

'It's Ru, the Supporter of the Sky!' they would shout.

'It was nothing, really. I've just come to check the stakes . . .'

But Maui grew tired of his father's visits and began to make fun of him.

'Ru, the Supporter of the Sky! Ru, the Bringer of Light! Ru, the Supporter of his own swollen head!'

'That's enough,' said Ru. 'A son should have respect for his father – as these people do, even though I did them only a little service. One more word from you, and you'll join the blue stone sky up there.'

'I dare you,' said Maui, and laughed in his face.

Without another word, Ru grabbed Maui and flung him like a pebble into the air. Maui bounced off the blue stone.

The islanders gazed at Maui tumbling towards the ground. But no! Where he had been there was now a bird soaring above them! No sooner a bird, but there was Maui again, towering over his father.

Maui seized Ru and threw him with such force that he smashed against the stony sky.

The islanders could hardly believe what they saw next. The blue stony sky was moving away and Ru was carried with it until he disappeared from their sight. He disappeared just like the smoke from their cooking fires which now rose straight into the air and melted away into the great space which had opened above them.

And every day now there were new wonders to see. The sun crept across the sky and was followed by the moon. At night, the sky was alive with starlight. Wind and rain were followed by sunshine and calm. There were so many changes, the islanders forgot Ru. Lifting the blue stone sky onto wooden stakes – what a poor thing that had been.

Polynesian

THE NORTH WIND AND THE ZEPHYR

The North Wind is a lady and there was a time when she made up her mind to give up her single life and get married. She had her eye on Zephyr, who lived in the south, so she went to him and said directly:

'Zephyr, how would you like to be my husband?'

Now the last thing Zephyr wanted was to get married. He led a lazy, comfortable life which he didn't want anyone to disturb – especially a wife. He seemed to give the idea some thought, and then, half stifling a yawn, said:

'I don't think that would suit me, Lady North. I mean, what could you bring me as a dowry? You haven't got a penny to call your own.'

'No one insults me that way,' thought Lady North. 'I won't let that remark pass without an answer.' And she began to blow.

Three days and three nights she blew without stopping. Her breath carried with it the snow from the mountain tops in the north. Three days and three nights it snowed till the villages and fields had disappeared under a blanket that gleamed silver in the sun. Lady North turned to Zephyr:

'Here is the dowry that you said I didn't have. Is that enough silver for you?'

And without another word, Lady North went off to rest.

Zephyr watched her go in silence. There was no howling, icy wind, or raging snowstorm from him. He just stared at the sparkling, silvery landscape, shrugged his shoulders, and began to blow. Three days and three nights he blew without stopping. His breath carried with it the heat which shimmered over the desert sands of the south. Three days and three nights it scorched till every trace of snow had melted away from the fields and villages.

So there was a shock waiting for Lady North when she woke up. All her dowry was gone. She rushed off to Zephyr but this time he was ready for her:

'Where did all your dowry go, Lady North?' he asked mockingly. 'Do you still want me to be your husband?'

'Me marry you? A man who can fritter away the whole of my dowry in three days? Certainly not!'

And she turned her back on him for ever.

Italian

FIRE MAKES HIMSELF A WIFE

In the days when the gods still lived on earth, only one of them lived alone – Kanya the god of Fire. He lived alone in his hut at the top of a rocky crag, but he did come down from time to time to amuse himself by setting the forests on fire.

Kanya wasn't sad or lonely because he had one thought which burned in his fiery brain: 'I, Kanya, am the most handsome, the most attractive of all the gods.'

Every morning, he went down to the pool which lay in the valley below his hut to admire his reflection in the water. There was so much to admire. There was his huge pear-shaped body and his two heads on ostrich necks – each head with its single glowing yellow eye. There were his seven arms to flex and stretch. There were the red hot claws of his three feet to manicure and trim – dainty feet, two like an ostrich's and one like a rheumatic elephant's.

Yes, Kanya was hideous – with a body made of half-molten lava. Birds fell stricken out of the sky when they smelled him pass below them.

But even Kanya loved something more than himself. One day his pool was visited by the goddess Ma. Kanya hid as she splashed her silvery arms and legs in the water: 'I shall capture her – how can she resist my looks?' The next moment the pool was a cauldron of boiling water and steam as Kanya waded in, his seven arms flailing. One look and Ma was gone.

So Kanya lost Ma but his vanity burned even more fiercely: 'Why do I need to bother with goddesses? I'll make a wife.'

That is what he did. When the time came to breathe life into her, he blew twice into her open mouth.

Her eyelids fluttered, her eyes opened and she screamed.

'Don't be frightened, wife, I am your husband, Kanya.'

'You are so . . . so ugly!' she wailed.

Kanya began to rage and bubble. 'You are looking at the most handsome creature in the whole universe! Come, a little kiss for your husband!'

'Never, you're a monster!'

Those were her last words. Kanya's fire destroyed his first attempt.

He was in such a rage that something went wrong with his recipe in his second attempt. The result was a purple woman with four legs and six arms but still she shrieked:

'Let me sleep again, you hideous nightmare!'

'Hideous nightmare! Take a look at yourself!' And Kanya squashed her flat.

At the third attempt, Kanya made a yellow woman and he named her Oananua. She was wise: although, since Kanya made her, who knows how that could be? On waking and seeing him, she fought down her fear – even when Kanya reached out to touch her.

'My gracious, handsome lord and master, I am still too weak to bear your touch. Your highness, please allow your humble servant a little time to gather her strength.'

Kanya sputtered and smouldered with joy. He left Oananua and went down to the pool for just one more look at those feet, those arms, those heads.

Kanya returned, smoking and spitting sparks, but Oananua had gone. Down the crag she had run, into the safety of the forests. She ran and ran until she came to the mountains and there she hid herself very carefully.

Looking down she could see

the fool Kanya raging and roaring after her, careless of everything in his path. Here the forest exploded into flame, there a line of fire raced through the grasslands leaving them blackened and smoking. Until Kanya's rage had burned itself out, she knew he would never find her.

Bantu

THE SPARK

It was night and Vainamoinen was trying to sleep. At least, he thought it was night – there was no way of telling. Eyes open, eyes closed, it made no difference. There was no moonlight to spread shadows in his room, no yellow sunlight to shoot through the cracks in his wooden shutters. There was no firelight to send shadows dancing. All was lost – Sun, Moon, and Fire – stolen by his old enemy, Louhi, and carried off by her in a fiery bundle to the cold mountains of the north.

High above him in the clouds, a Sky Maiden had seen light disappear from the earth. Quickly she had kindled a spark, and cupping it in her windy hands she had placed it in a cloud cradle.

'When you grow I'll make you into a new sun and a new moon . . .'

She sang a spark lullaby while she rocked it to and fro, to and fro . . . oh! Too hard. Too late . . . the spark was falling to the earth, a tail of fire flaring out behind it.

The rush and the glare of the fire lit up Vainamoinen's room.

'That could be our stolen fire. I must see where it lands.'

Vainamoinen stumbled outside to the lakeside where he launched his boat. Only the sound of the lapping waves broke the black silence.

'Where are you going?' A new sound, soft and sighing, filled his straining ears. 'Vainamoinen, my son, I am the Water Mother.'

'Mother, I have lost the Moon, the Sun and the Fire. I think a piece of our fire has just fallen from the sky. Did you see where it landed?'

'Oh, that fire! Look no further! Not content with roaring through the forest and flickering over the marshes it came to boil my lake. The fish escaped to the shore and lay panting for their lives until one brave little fish leaped back into the boiling water and swallowed the fire. It darted about in pain straight into the mouth of a trout. Round and round the trout swam – the fish and the fire in his belly – until he was swallowed by a hungry pike. And now the pike is thrashing and gulping about the lake.'

In a moment, Vainamoinen cast his net into the water. When he pulled it in, it was bulging with fish, and there, still thrashing and gulping, was the pike. One knife cut and there was the trout. One more and there was the little fish. One more . . . but the fire had already flared across the water and crackled into the forest.

The fire gave Vainamoinen a long hard chase. Then suddenly it blazed up in front of him, waiting while Vainamoinen recovered enough breath to speak:

'Now fire, this is no way to go on for a fellow as bright as you – you're homeless and have no place to go. Why not come back with me where you can have a good hearth to live in and plenty of work to keep you happy?'

As it thought things over, the fire flared up again, and then died away. It smouldered contentedly when Vainamoinen carefully picked it up and put it in his tinder box.

Back home, Vainamoinen sat by his blazing hearth and looked hard into the fire. Outside, the firelight pushed back the darkness a little.

Finnish

THE GREAT FIRE

Long ago, there was a war between the tribes of the land of Yurakara. It does not matter how it began. There was no one left alive who remembered that. At first they had fought with slings and stones. Then clever men in one tribe had invented spears that flew straight to their target. So the other tribe must have spears, and their men learned to coat their arrow tips in poison.

So it went on until a time when the whole land was parched by a great drought. Even the fighting stopped – it was too hot to move. Both sides were angry at this but no one was more angry than Sararuma, an evil spirit who hated all people.

He visited the chiefs of both tribes and gave them the same advice:

'Now is your chance. Set fire to the grasslands and the forests and your enemies will be destroyed.'

No one recognised Sararuma or asked him who he was. How could they? He spoke the words they wanted to hear.

It was so easy – one spark struck and the fire raced through the grasslands and roared through the forests. The fire took no sides –

it burned everything and spared no one.

No one, that is, except one man and his wife. They had seen how it would all end and they had dug a deep pit in the earth and hidden themselves.

After the fire had burned itself out there was only silence. When the man could bear it no longer he cautiously poked a long twig out of the pit but it exploded into flame. The man waited a full day before trying again. This time there was no flame but when he pulled the twig back the end was blackened and a lurid red glow was travelling fast towards his hand. On the third day, when the man pulled back the twig the end was cold and grey. So he climbed out of the pit.

'Can you see anything?' his wife called. But the man did not answer and when she climbed out she understood why.

As they stood together, they saw what seemed to be a red flame twisting across the blackened earth

towards them. It was Sararuma
wrapped in his red flame cloak.

'Do you like your new home?'
Sararuma taunted.

'Yes,' said the man, and his
wife nodded.

Sararuma's flaming cloak paled
and, at their feet, grassblades, a
vivid green, pushed through the
ashes.

'You think this won't all
happen again? You want to live to
see that?' yelled Sararuma

'We want to live,' said the
wife.

Sararuma's cloak paled again
and through it the man and his wife
could see new leaves covering the
charred trees.

'All alone?' Sararuma said.

'Not forever.'

'We shall have children.'

Then a cooling wind rose
which swirled about Sararuma
putting out his pale fire and
blowing away his words.

South American

THE DROUGHT

It stopped raining.

The last rain was green and black, warm and sticky; it steamed off the earth, and the air was thick and green with thunder.

Then it stopped. The sun began to bleach the sky as white as a bone.

Tiddalick the giant frog winked an eye. The cool shadow of his rock dwindled to a ragged scrap, his green-brown skin twitched and steamed. He was thirsty. He was dreaming of sweet water, scented with flowers, fanned by breezes as light as a bird's wing, rippling, gushing. He opened his mouth – the air was dry as a bone.

Tiddalick set out in search of a drink.

His lopsided shadow fell across the lazy river, and dipping his mouth to the water he began to drink. With mud-green eyes he gazed into the distance while the river and all its straw and mud and weed poured down his throat with a rattling of small stones. He drank on and on until there was nothing left but black mud in the river bed; and then sorrowfully he belched.

He was still thirsty.

He drank a lake.

He was still thirsty.

He drank all the dirty ponds, all the shrinking streams, all the waterholes he could find, all the water that was left, until he was so swollen with water that he couldn't move.

And it wouldn't rain. The sky crackled and the earth smoked with dust.

All the people and birds and animals were gathered with their eyes fixed on Tiddalick's swollen belly, slopping with water. If only he would open his mouth, and let just a little of it out . . .

Kangaroo and Kookaburra tried to make him laugh.

'Ha ha ha! Ha ha ha!' cackled Kookaburra. His feathers were dull, and clung to him in lumps. 'Look at you! You bloated frog! You water-skin! You inflated bag of skin and bone! How long are you going to sit holding your breath, fatty?'

Kangaroo told him funny stories. Tiddalick's deep wet green eyes only swam round slowly in their sockets. Once he belched mournfully, and a dribble of water spilled out of his mouth and down his chin.

Kangaroo's throat was too dry to go on.

'Ha ha ha! Falling asleep, potbelly?' screeched Kookaburra desperately. 'Dozy! Dopey!'

But first one eye then the other eye shut, like green lights going out.

'Laugh! Laugh!' yelled Kookaburra.

Birds and animals and people all feebly flapped and waved their arms and squawked and staggered up to dance. No one smiled.

Noyang the Eel bit his tail and turned himself into a hoop. Grimly he bowled about, then unwound himself in the dust in front of Tiddalick and began wriggling and writhing madly. He bit the dust, whipped himself, twisted faster and faster.

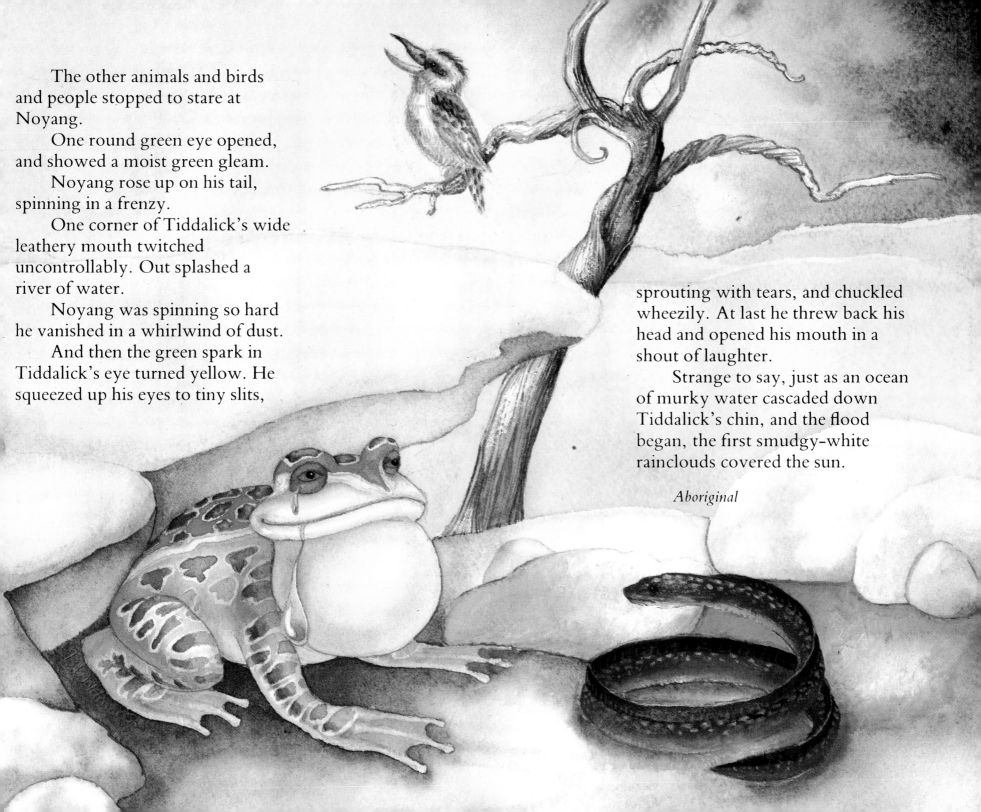

The other animals and birds and people stopped to stare at Noyang.

One round green eye opened, and showed a moist green gleam.

Noyang rose up on his tail, spinning in a frenzy.

One corner of Tiddalick's wide leathery mouth twitched uncontrollably. Out splashed a river of water.

Noyang was spinning so hard he vanished in a whirlwind of dust.

And then the green spark in Tiddalick's eye turned yellow. He squeezed up his eyes to tiny slits, sprouting with tears, and chuckled wheezily. At last he threw back his head and opened his mouth in a shout of laughter.

Strange to say, just as an ocean of murky water cascaded down Tiddalick's chin, and the flood began, the first smudgy-white rainclouds covered the sun.

Aboriginal

BEEBYEEBYEE AND THE WATER GOD

What was there for a woman to do all day? Digging roots, carrying water from the river, pounding fufu corn, and when the men came back from the river, there were their fish to grill for them . . .

Beebyeebyee stamped her brown foot and clenched her white teeth. What a pretty girl she was! But she would not do what her mother told her. She would not dig roots, carry water, pound corn; and she wanted to eat fish herself.

'How will I ever get you a husband?' cried her mother.

'I'll find one for myself,' said Beebyeebyee.

She took her canoe out on the river, and paddled upstream, away from where the men were fishing. When the thumping and the chanting from beside the women's huts grew fainter, Beebyeebyee rested her paddle and leaned her arms on the side of the canoe, looking down into the water. A shadow moved on the river bed; she thought it was a big fish, until it swam up and up, and out of the water beside her burst a young man, gleaming, and silver-grey, smiling with teeth like pearls: a Water God.

Now what was there for Beebyeebyee to do all day except play with him, swimming and diving and kissing and laughing until she was tired? And before long the Water God made her his wife, and he sent her back to the village with her canoe piled high with fish.

Every day she brought the villagers plenty to eat, enough for the men and the women too. And when they had eaten it all, they wondered how a girl, a weak thoughtless girl, could have caught so many fish. The most experienced fishermen never filled their boats so full as Beebyeebyee's. The men began to be angry and jealous.

Some of the young men followed Beebyeebyee to where she had found her Water God. They saw her lean over the water and sing to him, they saw him rise out of the water, silver-grey and gleaming; and Beebyeebyee and her Water God played and swam together until she was tired. Then he filled her canoe with fish and she paddled home.

The young men returned to the place; leaning over the water they sang Beebyeebyee's song, and when the Water God swam up

beside the canoe they caught him and killed him.

The next day Beebyeebyee called and called over the water, but her Water God never answered. Then what was there for her to do all day but cry until her eyes were red, and go home in the evening with her canoe empty?

'No luck today?' jeered the men.

But that night the river burst its banks and flooded the village: it covered every house and drowned all the people.

Except for Beebyeebyee: and she married the Water God's brother.

Cameroon

THE STORM

Once a rich mandarin was making a long sea voyage when a great storm blew up. The night was pitch black and the waves were mountain high. No boat could weather such a storm. The mandarin went on deck and held on grimly, straining to see through the darkness but knowing what must come. Then out of the darkness shone a bright point of light. It moved ahead of the boat and guided it safely to a small island.

'This light . . . which one of you? I owe my life . . .' gasped the merchant to the island people who had rescued him.

'No sir, you owe us nothing. It was the lantern of the Lin maiden you saw. She watches over those at sea.'

They took off his drenched clothes and gave him dry ones, and as he dozed by their warm fire they continued:

'You see, sir, it happened like this. Hundreds of years ago, on the shore of the eastern sea, there lived a fisher family named Lin: a father, a mother, two sons, and a daughter – and such a daughter, known and loved along the whole coast. She was up first every morning to make breakfast for her parents. Then down to the sea with her father and brothers to help prepare the boats and nets. Every morning as they launched their boats against the incoming waves they heard her call, 'Good wind and good weather!'

'Sir, you're beginning to dream by that warm fire, and perhaps it's the storm which fills your mind. That's how it was with the Lin maiden. She had been working with her mother one day. They'd had their midday meal and as she sat she began to feel sleepy, and slept, and dreamed a strange dream.

'She dreamed of the five dragon brothers who live beneath the sea. Something had made them angry – and when they are angry, and lash their mile-long tails, mountains collapse into the sea and waves touch the sky.

'The fierce storm raged in her dream, and there, tossed about in their little boats, she saw her father and her brothers. She rushed to the seashore and waded into the water, and somehow she caught hold of the rope fastened to the bows of her father's boat. Holding this rope in her teeth she seized the ropes tied to her brothers' boats and began to pull them all to safety.

'Just then, her mother tried to

wake her. "Daughter! Daughter!"

'The Lin maiden opened her mouth to answer, and in her dream the rope slipped from between her teeth and her father's boat disappeared under the waves.

'All through the afternoon, far into the evening, mother and daughter sat waiting, for what they knew must come. Only two brothers returned. "Our father's boat has been lost. He has gone to the Sea Dragon's Palace."

'The Lin maiden said nothing. She ran past her brothers and out of the house, down to the seashore; and there she plunged into the water to seek for her lost father . . .

'They never found the body, sir. But her brothers and other sailors started to see her out at sea, in the fiercest storms. No sailor who sees her is ever lost. They come safely to shore, as you did tonight, sir, with the help of her lantern.'

Chinese

THE STORY OF STORIES

Can you imagine a world without stories? I don't mean a world without books – stories came long before books. All of the stories in this collection were told and passed on by word of mouth, from generation to generation, for thousands of years before they were written down. Most of them were first written down just when they were no longer being told – in many cases, because the peoples who told them had been destroyed or scattered, in others, because there was no new generation to pass them on to.

But a world without stories . . . what would people say if they didn't tell stories? For most of what they say is just that – what I did, what I saw, what I said when, have you heard, did you know . . . We're telling our own story and other people's all the time.

And what power there is in those stories. They can make you stop what you're doing, forget where you are, excite you, sadden you . . . anything. They can make you 'change your mind'.

There aren't many stories about *stories* – what difference they make, how important they can be to individuals or whole nations. Here is one – it was told by the Seneca Indians of North America. Like all good stories it can speak for itself but like all good stories it also asks a question and one so important that everyone in this story asks it – 'What does it mean to tell stories?'

Poyeshao's mother and father died when he was only a few weeks old. Another woman brought him up and gave him his name, Poyeshao, which means orphan.

His foster mother told him when he was old enough that if he took out his bow and arrows, and hunted for birds, and became in time a good hunter, he would never want for anything in this world. Poyeshao took his bow and arrows into the woods, and every time he was tempted to stop hunting and rest, he remembered his foster mother's advice.

The first evening and the second evening he came home with a good string of birds. His foster mother was full of praise for him. The third day and the fourth day he worked even harder, and his foster mother had so many birds she was able to give some away to her neighbours. So it went on for nine days.

On the tenth day, at about midday, the sinews which held his feathers to his bow became loose, and Poyeshao looked for a place where he could sit and fix it. He came to a green clearing in the woods, with, in the middle of it, a smooth, round, flat-topped rock; he clambered up, sat down on the warm stone and set to work.

'Unwind the sinew . . . soften it in my mouth . . . rearrange the feathers; by tonight I should have found, if this does not delay me too long, more birds than ever before . . .'

'Shall I tell you stories?'
Poyeshao looked up, startled,

but no one had come into the clearing so he went back to his work. 'Rewind the sinew . . .'

'Shall I tell you stories?'

Perhaps someone was playing a trick on him? Poyeshao sat and looked and listened.

'Shall I tell you stories?' The voice was coming from the stone!

'What does it mean – to tell stories?' Poyeshao asked.

'It is telling what happened a long time ago, in the world before this one. Let me have your birds and I'll tell you stories.'

Poyeshao hesitated. 'All my birds?'

The stone was silent.

'Here, you can have them,' said Poyeshao hastily. 'Tell me . . .'

So the stone began, and it told stories until nightfall. Not that Poyeshao noticed the night fall – all that mattered was the stories.

'We will rest now,' said the stone at last. 'Come again tomorrow.'

Poyeshao went home, with only two or three birds to show his foster mother.

'I've killed so many; they're getting scarce,' he told her – that night, and the next, and the one after that . . .

'He used to be such a good boy,' she complained to her neighbours. 'He never idled his time away. But now . . .'

And she hired a boy to follow Poyeshao.

Poyeshao seemed in such a hurry; he scarcely stopped to pick up the birds he shot along the way. As he came near to the clearing, he broke into a run, and the boy, stumbling after, heard the sound of voices: yet there, when he found him, perched up on top of his stone, he seemed to be quite alone. The boy was too curious to hide.

'What are you doing up there?'

'Hearing stories.'

'Stories? What are they?'

'Jump up on the stone and listen.'

And again the stone told them stories until nightfall.

'I did follow him,' said the boy to Poyeshao's foster mother. 'We hunted together all afternoon. But there aren't many birds left. We're going out together again tomorrow, to see if we can find a few more.'

The woman was doubtful. She sent two men to follow the boys, and the next day they tracked them to the clearing. They watched the boys jump onto the stone, and when they heard a voice they came out of hiding behind the trees.

'What are you doing, boys?'

'Do you promise you won't tell anyone?' asked Poyeshao. The men promised.

'Now jump up and sit on the stone . . . Go on with the story, we are listening.' All the afternoon and into the evening Poyeshao, the boy and the two men sat listening, and when at last the stone sent them home, it told them that the next day they must bring all the people in the village to listen to the stories.

Next morning, when all of them were sat down in the clearing around the stone, and all of them were quiet, the stone spoke:

'I will tell you stories of what happened long ago. There was a world before this and what I shall tell you happened there. Some of you will remember every word I

say, some only a part, and some of you will forget them all. You must do the best that you can. Now listen.'

Every man, woman and child was silent and listened. Their silence was only broken by an occasional deep sigh. For three days the people listened in the clearing, and then late in the afternoon of the third day the stone said:

'I have finished. Keep these stories as long as the world lasts. Tell them to your children and your grandchildren. Those of you who

forget, ask for the stories from those who remember. I know all that happened in the world before this, and I have told it to you. Now I have finished.'

And so it was from the stone that the Senecas gained all their knowledge of the world before this.

. . . 'all their knowledge of the world before this'? Or simply our own world transfigured and fascinating, as if they had never known it before?